For Marianne, Jon
and their Grandma and Grandpa

First published in Great Britain in 2012 by Sheepsy Ltd.
Text and illustrations copyright © Joseph Theobald 2012

Joseph Theobald asserts his moral right to be identified
as the author and Illustrator of this work

ISBN 978 0 9572791 0 0

British Library CIP data availabe

Additional graphics by Martin Davis Still-Moving
Printed in on FSC certified paper by Indigo Press, UK

10 9 8 7 6 5 4 3 2 1

Marvin and Molly

Joseph Theobald

SHEEPSY

Marvin and Molly loved to play together
all day long. They would run, jump,
climb up hills and roll down again.

Marvin loved being silly to make Molly laugh.
They were best friends.
"I'm a mud monster!" roared Marvin.

But one day Molly saw Marvin in a different way.
She thought Marvin was the most handsome
sheep that she had ever seen.
Molly wanted to marry Marvin!

She tried to look
pretty for Marvin,
but Marvin didn't notice...

She gave Marvin flowers,
but Marvin just gobbled them up!

She wanted to cuddle Marvin,
but Marvin only wanted to climb up a tree.

Molly didn't know what to do.

The next day Molly was nowhere to be found.
"Where's Molly?" asked Marvin.
"Baaaaaaaa," said the other sheep.

Finally, Marvin found Molly
but she was not alone...

Molly had a new best friend!

"Come and play!" said Marvin.
But Molly didn't want to play anymore.
Molly's new best friend had some special things...
Maybe that's why Molly likes him, thought Marvin.

Marvin felt very sad. He left the meadow
and went to the woods to be alone.
"I wish I had some special things too,"
grumbled Marvin.

In the middle of the night Marvin woke up.
There were strange lights and strange
sounds coming through the trees.
Feeling brave, he went to have a closer look...

"Woooooooah!" gasped Marvin.
He had never seen anything like it!
"I will find lots of special things down there!"
Marvin went to see what he could find.

He found some special boots...

He watched people dance with their best friends...

Then he met some children
who gave him lots of special things!

They even brushed his wool.
Marvin felt very special indeed.

Marvin found his way back to the meadow.
He wanted to show Molly how good he
looked with all his special new things...
Marvin had a plan!

He **danced** and **danced** like he
had never danced before!
He sang a little song for Molly!

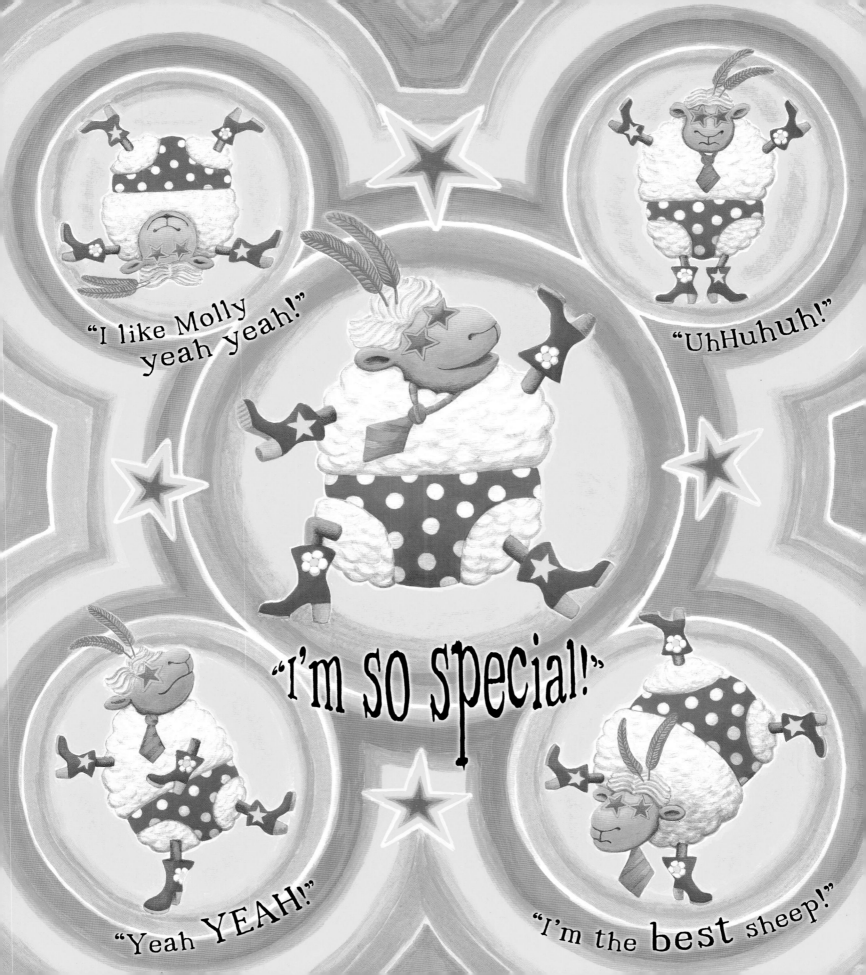

But Marvin had been so busy dancing that he hadn't noticed all the sheep laughing at him... All except for Molly.

"That was **amazing!**" said Molly. "You are the most special sheep ever, with or without those special things".

HA HA HA

HA HA HA

BAA HA HA HA HA!

Marvin and Molly were best friends again.
That night they cuddled under their favourite
tree and looked up at the stars.

"Will you marry me?" asked Marvin.
"Yes," said Molly. "When we are grown up.
But first lets play lots of silly games together!"

...and they did.

Also available as a vibrant, interactive, animated App!

Also by
Joseph Theobald

Available for Apple
and Android devices.

For further information,
competitions and more,
visit Marvin and Molly's
Sheepsy website

Help Marvin practice his
good manners with this
fun FREE App!

SHEEPSY

Can **you** draw the best dressed sheep?

Use the picture frame above to draw
your own dressed-up sheep!

Send Marvin and Molly **your pictures** online
and see them on Marvin the Sheep's
'Best dressed sheep' gallery on Facebook

For details, competitions and more
visit the **'fun-stuff'** page at
www.sheepsy.com or find
'Marvin the Sheep' on Facebook